The Outbreak of a Monstrous Infection

Afshan Naheed Hashmi,
PhD, C(ASCP), RAC

ISBN(paperback): 978-1-7358117-1-0
ISBN(e-book): 978-1-7358117-2-7; mobi:978-1-7358117-3-4
Printed in the United States of America,2019
Published by: Dr Afshan Hashmi Consulting Group, LLC

"No dream is too big. No challenge is too great. Nothing we want for our future is beyond our reach."
—President Donald J. Trump

My creativity has increased several times since President Trump has taken office. As now, during the Presidency of President Trump, I feel very safe and healthy in America. This book is also dedicated to all the Americans and to the movement:
"Make America Great Again" #MAGA

Thanks a lot, President Trump, for inspiring me as well as being the best President of America I have encountered in my life. May God Almighty always Bless you with His Choicest Blessings. Amen as well as Ameen!

Dedication:

With lots of love, I dedicate this book to the loving memory of my
Maternal Grandparents: *Prof. Abdul Aleem & Mrs. Ismat Aleem*
my **Maternal Great-Aunt:** *Shafqat, lovingly called Gaga and*
My Parents,
Mom: *Mrs. Jamila Siddiqi,*
Dad: *Prof. A. Majid Siddiqi,*
my **Maternal Aunt:** *Waseema Hashim and*
my **Younger Brother:** *Faizi*

Acknowledgements:

Writing is a passion I have pursued since childhood. Science fiction is a genre that is universally liked. Being a scientific entrepreneur, I thought to dive into this genre. I hope this book is liked by a lot of people and that will encourage me to write even more in this genre.

First of all, I thank God Almighty for His blessings. It is through Him that all things are possible, and my book is possible because of my Almighty Lord.

I want to thank President Trump for inspiration and the wonderful books President Trump has written. You have always inspired me since childhood. Every day while writing this book I have followed you on print, online and social media platforms. Your policies have given me an inspiring way to think with more creativity and innovation. Elegant, caring and beautiful First Lady Melania Trump I love to follow, what you wear. I am so lucky to live in a time when I got a chance to see President Trump as President of the United States of America and Melania Trump as my First Lady. I love you both a lot. Seeing you both on television makes me very happy and it increases my creativity.

This book is also dedicated to all the Americans and to the movement:

"Make America Great Again" #MAGA

I would especially like to thank my first teachers and mentors in my life, my maternal grandparents Prof. Abdul Aleem & Mrs. Ismat Aleem , my maternal Great-Aunt Shafqat, lovingly called Gaga , my mom Jamila Siddiqi, my dad Prof. A. Majid Siddiqi and my maternal aunt Waseema Hashim. These all great individuals, have always loved me more than themselves, raised me like a princess, and encouraged and supported me, in whatever I liked to do. They have implanted in me lot of confidence, which helps me to face any situation that life puts in front of me. They have taught me everything about life. My younger brother, Faizi for always supporting and loving me a lot. Although they all are not with me today, I know they must be watching from Heaven, and their noble teachings will always guide me. I miss them a lot.

I am indebted to my husband, Mustafa Hashmi. I love you, honey. Mustafa is my first reader, and without his love and encouragement as well as belief in the project, I could not have written this book. My handsome husband, who walked arm in arm with me throughout this project.

I am truly blessed and thankful to my family and friends who have always encouraged me to write this book. I am thankful to my older brother, Dr. Shahid Jameel, for always encouraging me. To the many friends who made me laugh even when I felt like crying and kept me on track for years it took to write this book who are mentioned here. There were some days when I was tired and then my friends who are like sisters to me Zia Afroz Naqvi, Erka Syed, Samina Ahmad, Asma Qureshi, Irma Hafeez and Parveen Siddiqui talked to me, and were always there for me. Also, I want to thank my two sweet cousins Shazma Habib and Nabila Faruqi who always encouraged me, during the highs and lows of the entire book development process.

I do not have words to express my feelings of gratitude and happiness to all of these very high achievers and busy people for caring about my success and taking time from their busy schedules to provide me with a endorsements/blurbs/comments/reviews for "The Outbreak of a Monstrous Infection". These wonderful, charming, and highly successful thought leaders, who believed in my vision and writing philosophies and wrote praise for The Outbreak of a Monstrous Infection.

Excellent writing of lovely, sparkling, inspiring and exquisite words. and Shining Endorsements/blurbs/comments/reviews of "The Outbreak of a Monstrous Infection" by:

Ambassador Dr. Har Swarup Singh former Vice- Chancellor (President) Haryana State Agricultural University, India, former Member of India's Planning Commission (in the rank of a Central Minister of State); former Governor of Pondicherry; and India's Former Ambassador to the beautiful island nation of Maldives; worked with the United Nations for over two decades, rising to the position of Director in the U.N. System and then Deputy Executive

Director of a leading inter-governmental group: International Cotton Advisory Committee, Washington, D.C., Currently busy with think tank activities, community service, traveling, and writing.

Nilima Mehra, by profession is a Biochemist (McGill University, Montreal, Canada). She has been a professor at Penn State University. She was the chief Biochemist at Ayerst Pharmaceuticals in Montreal, Canada. Nilima with Dr. Stein has authored scientific research papers. She has been in media, both on Radio & TV, for over the past 44 years. Nilima is the first Indian American (Executive Producer Of GTV, Washington, DC.) to Broadcast her TV productions on a National TV ; FOX 5. "Nilima Mehra has been hailed as one of the most glamorous and elegant personality's in the Nation's Capital Area" says Aziz Haniffa of India Abroad who also calls her a role model for the young girls, women & women entrepreneurs." Nilima is a dedicated humanitarian & has carved a special path for women to follow" said Ambassador Siddhartha Shankar Ray of India to the US. Nilima is also a philanthropist. She supports 75 organizations globally.

Also, I am very disappointed with some people who promised me to give endorsements, but refused at the last moment because I have supported President Trump. I have lost many friends for supporting President Trump and to them I say "I do not care." You were not my true friends. I will always stand for right thing and that's what I did by supporting President Trump and his policies.

<u>Character List</u>:

Dr. Honey Singh: Medical doctor and director of a medical institute in USA

Baby Singh: Dr. Honey Singh's wife

Dr. Michael Singh: Medical doctor in India and Baby Singh's father

Dr. Kathleen Singh: Medical doctor and only daughter of Dr. Honey and Baby Singh

Queen Saba: Queen of UAE

His Majesty Sulaiman: King of UAE

Dr. Happy Singh: Nephew of Dr. Honey Singh and adopted son of Dr. Honey Singh and director of blood bank in USA

Mitra Singh: Elder brother of Dr. Honey Singh and biological father of Dr. Happy Singh

Helen Singh: Younger sister of Baby Singh and manager of office of Dr. Honey Singh

Dr. Rosilina (Rozy) Singh: Medical doctor and daughter of Helen Singh

Nancy Goldstein: Attorney of Dr. Honey and Baby Singh

Michelle Goldstein: Attorney and daughter of Nancy Goldstein

Dr. Jack Singh: Medical doctor in USA and husband of Rosilina Singh

Ms. Lilly Flowers: Secretary in office of Dr. Honey Singh

Sunita and Ranveer Singh: Dr. Jack Singh's parents and owner of bookstore in New Delhi, India

Protima Singh: Cousin of Helen Singh and socialite in Page-3/ elite circles in India

Renu Jaiswal: Famous wedding planner in India

Dr. Balwant Singh: CEO of hospital in India and cousin of Dr. Honey Singh

Dr. Bubleen Cozee Singh: Medical doctor and elder brother of Dr. Jack Singh

Dr. Sudha Cozee Singh: Medical doctor and wife of Dr. Bubleen Cozee Singh

Ms. Angelina Gold: Owner of famous PR firm in USA

Shilpa Darling: Choreographer of Bollywood

Pamela Singh Fashion icon in India

Dr. Seva Shanti: Medical doctor and one of the best friends of Dr. Bubleen Cozee Singh

Angela Paul: Hollywood actress

Nisha Thakur: Celebrity henna designer

Seema and Gita: Daughters of Dr. Bubleen Cozee Singh

Dr. Nishi Talwar: Medical doctor and lover of Dr. Seva Shanti

Dr. Indu Mehra: Cousin of Dr. Nishi Talwar and medical doctor

Her Excellency Pheroza Motiwala: President of India

Dr. Mushir Lakhanwala: Prime Minister (PM) of India

Misha Singh: Famous designer

Meenakshi Devi: Famous Bollywood star

Jisma Gomez: Hollywood actress

Karen Moore: Lead FBI agent

Sheila Motwani: Lead CBI agent

Milan Chaudhry: A person living in UAE

Sujan Jhunjunwala: Underworld King of Dubai, UAE

Miland Thappar: Associate of Sujan Jhunjunwala

Shridan: Associate of Sujan Jhunjunwala

Sheena Kulkarni: Wife of Miland Thappar

Aabheer and Mrs. Norain Gupta: Power couple

Girdhari Sharma: Fan of Bollywood actress Meenakshi Devi

Anuj Pratap: Fan of Bollywood actress Meenakshi Devi

Durdana Singh: Partner of Sujan Jhunjunwala

Kurt Shein: Attorney of Aabheer and Norain Gupta

Nikhil Saxsena: Attorney of Dr. Seva Shanti and Dr. Indu Talwar

Gia Gidwani: Spokesperson of Supreme Court of India

Martin Luizo: Celebrity chef

Liz Shaw: Hollywood actress

Jean Robert: Hollywood actress

Dr. Featherson: Chief researcher on developing Zika vaccine

Barbara Wilkenson: Famous documentary director in Hollywood

Steve Berger: Famous Hollywood producer

Chitra Singh and Taimur Singh: Children of Dr. Jack and Dr.Rosy Singh

Contents

Introduction: My Story – How *The Outbreak of a Monstrous Infection* Came to Be, by Dr. Afshan Naheed Hashmi xiv

About the Book: xvi

1964–2018 1

2018 Pre-Wedding Preparations 9

Meeting with a Best Friend 11

Henna and Music Night, Dec. 24, 2018 14

Wedding Day, Dec. 25, 2018 17

Mystery Illness 21

Manhunt for the Suspects 26

Funeral of PM and President of India, 2019 29

Buzz about a Power Couple 31

Absconding Culprits Found 35

Confession of Crimes and Convictions 37

After the Judgment of the Supreme Court of India 43

Multi-Million-Dollar Deals 45

Photo Gallery: Some magical moments that led to the birth of *The Outbreak of A Monstrous Infection* 46

About the Author: Dr. Afshan Naheed Hashmi 53

Thank You and Request to Readers to Give a Review for The Outbreak of A Monstrous Infection 54

Introduction: My Story – How *The Outbreak of a Monstrous Infection* Came to Be, by Dr. Afshan Naheed Hashmi

Dear Readers,

I want to thank President Trump for being the best president I have encountered in my life. His America First Agenda, "#Make America Great Again," is so good for we the silent majority who were suffering due to not having jobs and can now have jobs and freedom to do whatever we want. We feel a fresh breeze coming in our windows.

My story diving into the publishing world begins with that.

After 9/11, I and many other Muslims in America were always perceived as a potential threat to America when people came to know that we were Muslims. There are good and bad characters everywhere and in every religion. Believe me, I have seen the look given to me when I stood for long hours with my feet swelling in lines for interviews and finally my name came. Either the hiring officer left or did not come. All people of any caste, creed, color, religion, or ethnicity should unite together in today's world and try to kill the evils of society.

The idea to ponder is, "United we stand and divided we fall."

Under President Trump's presidency it's the dawn of a new era. I love the agenda of President Trump's "Peace through Strength."

I felt I had all the qualifications for a great job and future in America and came here for my American Dream thousands of miles from my luxurious life in India. I hated the corruption in

India and since my parents were here before my birth, they always told me about their nice experience in America and how everyone is treated equally. But without a job for so long and seeing people less qualified than me living their American Dream, I felt very frustrated in life. I trained so many people at a nice-paying job and the day the project was finished, I was told I no longer had the job. I heard in media stories that this was the case for many Americans and so we all voted for President Trump. But God is great and the patriotic Americans, irrespective of any caste, creed, and color, selected my favorite President Trump.

I always used to say since childhood that one day I would go to America and meet Mr. Donald J. Trump. But I never knew at that time that one day would dawn when he would help so many Americans like us who felt crushed in America by not having jobs.

Due to a boost in the economy and many positive steps being taken under the presidency of President Trump, I feel so good and safe in America, which I never felt before. When the right things start to happen things start falling in place.

Being a scientific entrepreneur by profession, I know what harm terrorism can cause.

This is a fiction story to educate people how terrorism can cause harm beyond imagination.

I am so thankful to President Trump for taking care of suspected chemical attacks in Syria.

There are many kinds of biological warfare agents. Biological warfare agents are a threat to the human population. Nobody should get their hands on them. Scientists working in various labs should be very careful as to how they dispose of these agents. Strict protocols should be in place in disposing these agents.

This story is an imagination cocktail I have**concocted** with my imagination. Everything written is fictional.

Enjoy reading the book,
Cheers!
Dr. Afshan Naheed Hashmi
www.afshanhashmi.com
www.drafshanhashmi.com

About the Book:

A monstrous infection is spreading worldwide. Is this a simple infection or a deliberate attempt to ruin the human population, or bio-terrorism? What is this global infection and who is spreading this? To know that, read this suspense-filled book by an Amazon best-selling and hot #1 new-release author of a previous book called *The Modern Mughal Mentality: New Strategies to Succeed in India and the Global Marketplace*. In the author's second book, a sizzling science-fiction story, a crime is investigated by the FBI in collaboration with the Central Bureau of Investigation (CBI) of India.

Chapter One:
1964–2018

In a sprawling bungalow in Potomac, Maryland, USA, lived Dr. Honey Singh, a board-certified internal-medicine and family-practice physician, along with his beautiful wife, Baby Singh. Baby Singh was a fashionista and was funding women's causes through her Honeybabe foundation. She had a ladies book club by the name of Baby's Glam and Glitzy Club, which had many glam and glitzy ladies who were professionals living in Washington, DC, Potomac, Maryland, Virginia, and even Beverly Hills, California, as well as elites from all of America, meeting at her place on the last Wednesday of every month discussing various aspects of charities they wanted her and Dr. Honey to fund. In this club there was a wide spectrum of career women. There were doctors, lawyers, actresses, business owners, and models, to name a few.

In these book-club meetings members would come prepared after reading a book of a famous woman author, and that author was even invited from any part of the world to give her presentation, followed by a Q-and-A in this prestigious and elite gathering. The book club was followed by a sumptuous meal, which was specially prepared by a celebrity chef with his or her specialty cuisine. Each month a different cuisine was tried by voting at the beginning of the year. This ladies club operated from March till November every year and authors around the world wanted to come and present their book in this club.

The Singh' s not only were doctors but also owned many media companies and hence were also media moguls. In the beginning of the year in January, the book was decided by a poll in which millions of fans of authors participated to get their favorite authors in this contest.

Baby Singh was the daughter of a famous doctor of New Delhi, India, Dr. Michael Singh, who had a roaring practice and owned several hospitals in Med City and several other destinations in India. Dr. Michael Singh was killed in a plane crash in October 2010. Baby, with blue eyes and very fair complexion, five feet ten inches in height, was a famous model in India. Baby was crowned Miss India in 1965 and Miss Universe the following year. She got married to Dr. Honey Singh in 1968, who belonged to the royal family of Punjab and inherited a lot of property from his ancestors. Dr. Honey and Baby Singh had a beautiful American-architecture bungalow with forty rooms with scenic views and beautiful lights throwing their charm on the landscape, enhancing its beauty even more. There was a waterfall and adjacent to the waterfall was a statue of Lord Buddha. The beautiful and picturesque landscaping was done by a famous Italian architect who had done many celebrity homes and who was very popular with Washington, DC, and Hollywood elites for his unique perspective on his craft. Dr. Honey and Baby Singh were also known for their philanthropic activities, and their foundation, Honeybabe Foundation, was providing funds to non-profits that were involved in women's causes, especially education of underprivileged girls in both the USA and India. They even contributed a lot of money to the Academy Foundation in Los Angeles, California, for funding movies to be made to enhance the cause of underprivileged girls. This couple was always invited to the Oscars and other prestigious awards, in both Hollywood and Bollywood as well as in the music industry.

They had only a daughter, named Kathleen Singh, who was USA-board-certified in not only family practice but also gynecology. Kathleen was lovingly called Kathy. She looked after the practice of family medicine with her father and had her gynecology practice in the same office in Potomac, Maryland, on River Road. Singh and Associates Inc. were one of the most famous doctor groups, not only in the USA but around the world. They had patients coming from around the globe. They were affiliated with the world-famous teaching hospital Rosen Medical Center in Bethesda, MD. Doc Kathy had treated a queen from the

UAE by the name of Saba who was suffering from infertility and then she had triplets. Her husband His Excellency Sulaiman and Her Excellency Queen Saba awarded her with one hundred million dollars and two private jets. Her Excellency Queen Saba and His Excellency Sulaiman were very happy with Doc Kathy for treating the infertility of Queen Saba.

Dr. Honey Singh had adopted one of his nephews, Happy Singh, from his elder brother Mitra Singh, who lived in Chandigarh, Punjab, and had twelve children, eight boys and four daughters. Dr. Honey Singh adopted Happy Singh when he was born in 1972 in Chandigarh and brought him to the USA. Dr. Happy Singh was now the director of a blood bank by the name of MedGoldStar Blood Bank in Washington, DC, and he too was a medical doctor, board-certified in internal medicine with special training in hematopathology as well as in blood bank/transfusion medicine. Both Kathleen and Happy studied in private school in Potomac, Maryland. They were raised in luxury with silver spoons in their mouths but were very dedicated children. Happy Singh did not know that he was adopted.

Baby Singh's younger sister, Helen Singh, had gotten divorced when she was very young and had one beautiful daughter who was thirty years of age and also a medical doctor board-certified in family practice, Rosilina Singh, lovingly called Rosy. She was also working in her uncle Dr. Honey Singh's practice. Helen was so disgusted with the idea of getting married that after her divorce she never thought of remarrying, although she'd gotten divorced at the age of twenty-five. Helen moved to the USA with her elder sister, Baby Singh, and was the manager of the office of Dr. Honey Singh.

Dr. Honey and Baby Singh had assets of one hundred billion in cash. They made a will that fifty billion would go to Kathleen, Dr. Happy would inherit twenty billion, Helen would inherit ten billion, Rosy would inherit ten billion, and ten billion would go to the charities who supported the education of underprivileged women. The only condition was that Kathy, Happy, Helen, and Rosy had to work till their last breath, as Dr. Honey and Baby did not want them to be spoiled by this extravagant amount of money they possessed. In case of any one of their deaths, their share would go to the Honeybabe Foundation. Kathy, Honey, Helen, and Rosy would be on the board of trustees of the Honeybabe Foundation, which had twenty employees.

Dr. Honey and Baby's lawyer, Nancy Goldstein, was the executor of the will, and she would be paid one billion from all these individuals before taking out any money that was assigned to them in the will. Nancy and her only daughter, Michelle Goldstein, who would inherit her law practice, would oversee this operation. Nancy had been a very loyal lawyer to Honey and Baby Singh since they arrived in the USA in 1970. Nancy had a roaring practice on K Street in Washington, DC, where her freshly graduated daughter Michelle had started working as a general-practice lawyer.

Helen completed her MBA degree from American University Business School in Washington, DC, in 1992. Helen's daughter met this very handsome young man from India named Dr. Jack Singh, who did his residency in family practice in the same medical school, Rosen Medical School in Bethesda, MD. Dr. Honey Singh was the medical director of this hospital. Jack did his schooling at the very prestigious Medical College All India Institute of Medical Sciences in New Delhi, India and stood first in his class. Dr. Rosy and Jack dated for three years and during the third year of their residency moved in together to see if they could put up with each other before getting married. One day both Jack and Rosy were very stressed out and came back from work and were sitting on the deck of their townhome in Fallsgrove in Rockville, Maryland. There was a full moon and a nice summery breeze with birds chirping near their window and all of a sudden, Rosy's feet touched Jack's feet and then Jack could not resist his feelings and started kissing Rosy, and then immediately took her in his lap to their beautiful bedroom, where light sitar music was playing, a very nice rose-scented candle was lit, and a wonderful painting of world-renowned Indian painter Maqbool Fida Husain hung above their bed, and they made their first love. There were bloodstains on the white sheet, which clearly indicated that Dr. Rosy was a virgin.

Now their relationship was going on to the next level. From now on in their live-in-relationship, they started making love with each other. After a month, Rosy skipped her menstrual period, and she was positive that she was pregnant. She told her secretary, Ms.

Lilly Flowers, that she was not feeling well. Dr. Rosy said, "Lilly, please reschedule all my appointments of the afternoon, either with Kathy or for another date, and I will take three days off." Dr. Kathy, her cousin, was also a partner in her internal-medicine practice, along with Dr. Honey Singh and Dr. Jack Singh. She then proceeded to the CVS drugstore on Rockville Pike in Rockville, MD, and immediately picked up a pregnancy-test kit to test her urine and find out whether she was pregnant or not. Rosy went home and did the pregnancy test and yes, she was right. Boom, she got the answer: she was pregnant. Her head was spinning and after taking two aspirin and sleeping for two hours, she called her cousin Kathy.

Rosy said, "Kathy, I want to meet you in Starbucks in Fallsgrove shopping center, right now."

Kathy said to Rosy, "Rosy, dear, you sound very tired. Is everything OK, honey? Should I bring Jack with me?"

Rosy screamed and said, "No Jack, only you. It's something very important but I cannot tell you on the phone."

Kathy, who had just finished seeing her last patient, immediately left her office, telling Ms. Flowers that she had some important errands to run and after that she would not come back to the office. It was 4:00 PM Eastern Time. By 4:30, Kathy reached Starbucks and there was Rosy, giving a very haggard look to Kathy and saying, "I am very sorry, Kathy, if I was rude to you earlier, I did not mean to react that way." She then whispered in Kathy's ear that she was pregnant. "I just took a urine test and am lost after finding the results."

Kathy asked, "Did you take the test with an over-the-counter kit available or through the Medshine Clinical Labs where we send our samples?"

Rosy replied, "I took it over-the-counter from the CVS drugstore. I feel very nauseated in the morning. But tomorrow I will go to the Medshine Clinical Chemistry Labs myself and get a stat test. Can you write me a stat-test referral form?"

Kathy said, "Sure."

First thing in the morning, Kathy ordered a stat pregnancy test for Rosy and faxed it to the lab. At 9:00 AM Rosy reached Medshine Labs on Travilah Road in Rockville, Maryland, and gave her blood for checking HCG levels to confirm pregnancy. HCG, or human chorionic gonadotropin, is a hormone made by the pregnancy that can be detected in the mother's blood or urine even before the woman's missed period. Two hours later, Kathy called Rosy and said, "Dear, you were right, it is confirmed that you are pregnant. Come to my office tomorrow, I want to do your first ultrasound."

Rosy then went home and slept again. Dr. Jack was working late for several days but when he heard that Rosy was off from work and was sick he went home early that day. When he reached home he asked, "Rosy, are you OK?"

Rosy became very emotional and said, "I am pregnant with your child. Are you going to marry me?"

Jack said immediately, "Of course, I love you, Honey, I will marry you. When do you want to get married? But the wedding reception has to take place in Chattarpur Farms, New Delhi, India, as my parents as well as most of my and your relatives live in India." Next Jack went out immediately to the Safeway market nearby in Fallsgrove Community Center and bought a bouquet of roses.

Also he went to the Democracy Boulevard Mall and went to Macy's and bought Rosy a beautiful diamond ring as well as a beautiful red gown with embroidery done intricately on the silk gown with sequins, pearls, and exclusive silk thread. The motifs done on the gown were depicting love and happiness ever after. Also Jack had ordered food from Barbeque Mission on Rockville Pike in Rockville, Maryland.

Jack said to Rosy, "We will have a court marriage here and once the reception is done in India, we will come back and give a grand reception here in Gaylord National Resort and Convention Center for this iconic wedding. Also we will charter a plane for one thousand guests from here to New Delhi if any of our relatives and friends want to come."

Rosy was very excited and said, "First we have to tell my mom, Helen, Aunt Baby, and Uncle Honey. Also, I will share your idea of doing the first reception in New Delhi, India. Let's see what they say." Rosy went and told Helen, Baby, and Honey. Helen was astonished and in anguish to hear that her daughter was pregnant before the wedding, a custom not prevalent in India. So many emotions were running through her mind. How would she tell her relatives in India, as some were living in a small village of Punjab called Kairon? Some of her relatives were very traditional and it would be a taboo for them to hear this news. So the wedding had to take place immediately.

Jack's parents, Sunita and Ranveer Singh, owned a wonderful bookstore in Connaught Place named Joy and Pride Bookstore. Connaught Place was one of the largest financial, commercial, and business centers in New Delhi, India. It was often known as CP and housed the headquarters of several noted Indian firms. The main commercial area of the new city, New Delhi, during the British Raj, Connaught Place occupied a place of pride in the city and was counted among the top heritage structures in New Delhi.

Joy and Pride Bookstore was a place of conversation. Communities used to gather there and talk about not only Indian but world politics. They had a coffee shop with delicacies and free Wi-Fi. The bookstore was decorated not only for Sikhs festival but also for Christmas, and you could see jingle bells and Christmas carols playing in the children's section of the bookstore. Mr. and Mrs. Santa Claus were sitting on their chair and a wonderfully decorated Christmas tree was behind them. The bookstore had a very big turnover every year of millions of dollars, in spite of the digital bookstores prevalent in India. Customers chatted over a cup of coffee and students were seen taking private lessons or doing their homework.

Helen called her cousin in New Delhi by the name of Protima Singh, who was very influential, to book one of Chatturpur Farms' beautiful properties by the name of ScenicView Retreat. The wedding venue could accommodate four thousand guests. So Protima, with her connections, booked the hotel for a winter wedding on December 25, 2018, Christmas Day. It was very difficult to get the whole hotel that day but Protima managed it somehow. Now, the Singhs wanted the invitations to be printed in India. So they hired a wedding planner by the name of Renu Jaiswal in India who was very popular in Page-3, or elite, circles. Renu ordered the invitations after getting them approved online by the Singhs. The invitations came with matching makeup kits from

Chanel consisting of an eyeliner, five lipsticks, foundation crème, and a powder, all with the initials of the bride and groom. They also came with matching boxes of Godiva chocolates with the initials of the bride and the groom. In gold letters R&J was embellished. They also came with iPads with a personalized welcome message from Honey, Baby, Helen, Rosy, and Jack to their guests.

Chapter Two:
2018 Pre-Wedding Preparations

The wedding was planned for Christmas Day and all the relatives of the Singhs were invited. There was a chartered plane from the USA to India that had the capacity of one thousand passengers, which included the friends of the Singhs, Helen, Kathleen, Rosy, and Jack. When they reached Indira Gandhi International Airport in New Delhi, there were gorgeous and beautiful girls waiting to receive them with beautiful red roses and gota, or shining thread garlands. The girls were wearing traditional Gota-Patti (shining thread and leaves) embroidered sarees. The sarees were in green and red, the Christmas colors. Also waiting for them were members of the international as well as Indian press. This wedding had been written about a lot in the press already. *Vogue India, Harper's Bazaar India*, and *Hello India* had already given the wedding a lot of publicity by writing about it since it was announced. Many in India's elite circles were talking if they could be guests at this billionaire doctor's niece's wedding.

The girls also had Aarti plates, a Hindu custom. Aarti was a Hindu religious ritual of worship, a part of *prayer* in which light from wicks soaked in ghee or purified butter or camphor was offered to one or more deities. Aartis also referred to the songs sung in praise of the deity when lamps were being offered. The girls performed the aarti with songs and then all the guests were directed towards the exit of the airport. Renu, the wedding planner, had arranged for their luggage to be taken directly to the Maurya

Sheraton Hotel. Luxurious buses from the hotel were waiting to transport the guests. There was a Lamborghini waiting exclusively for Rosy and Jack. Also present at the airport was the only elder brother of the groom, Dr. Bubleen Cozee Singh, who was assigned the task of receiving all the guests at the airport. The press was running after everyone to ask questions about the wedding, but the spokesperson of the wedding was a PR firm hired from America called Gold Art PR and the owner of the firm, Ms. Angelina Gold, along with ten of their one hundred employees, was also part of this wedding. Ms. Gold told the reporters that every day at 4:00 PM India Standard time till the day of the wedding, PR briefings would be done in the Golf Bar of the Maurya Sheraton Hotel with high tea every day. Gold Art PR employees who travelled to India were very proficient in Indian culture. They only catered to high-end Indian clients. All the guests who came from America in the chartered flight were staying in Maurya Sheraton Hotel.

Baby, Kathy, Helen, and Rosy had arranged to meet with the famous Italian designer Robert Medici, who was in India working with famous Indian designer Anil Sharma to create bridal-collection bags. Medici and Sharma collaborated to produce *Nawab, or royal,* jackets. These jackets were meant for the groom and all his friends looking for a royal touch in the grand Mehndi celebration, or Henna Night, to be held on December 24. Bags by Gucci, Canali hampers from Canali online store and scarves and ties from Salvatore Ferragamo were sourced by the hosts, Dr. Honey and Baby Singh, to give away as return gifts to the attendees at the wedding.

Also, a famous Bollywood choreographer by the name of Shilpa Darling was hired to teach all the family members some scintillating dance moves of Bollywood songs in both classic and contemporary styles. A fashion show was also arranged by a fashion icon of India, Pamela Singh. All the top models from around the world were hired and the theme was the Mughal emperors era of India with how they would look in modern times on the day of the wedding.

Chapter Three:

Meeting with a Best Friend

Dr. Bubleen Cozee Singh, lovingly known as Cozee, was also a very influential figure in elite circles of India. Everybody knew he did his residency at the same hospital where Dr. Honey Singh was the medical director before opening his private practice in New Delhi, India. As soon as Dr. Honey Singh saw him at the airport, he went green with anger as to how Dr. Cozee had come to receive him, because he had been fired by him on sexual harassment charges. He asked Jack, "Jack, how are you related to Dr. Cozee?" and Jack said, "He is my elder brother. I told you, sir, we are two brothers and Cozee is my elder brother."

Doc Honey had a gigantic ego and he made a big scene right there and said he could not let Rosy marry Jack, as this family was messed up, although Dr. Cozee had gone to rehab in the USA and had come clean of his dirty habit as a sexual predator and was now living a happily married life, with his wife, Dr. Sudha Cozee Singh, and two beautiful daughters, as well as a very successful career. Dr. Sudha knew that he'd gone to prison but believed everyone deserved a second chance in life. He was not a bad person, but he was sentenced to eight years in prison for his predator offense and deported to India on the condition that he could keep his medical license. His past was haunting him. He felt very humiliated but kept quiet for the sake of his younger brother, Jack.

The next day, Dr. Cozee received a call from Kathmandu, Nepal, from one of his best friends, Dr. Seva Shanti, who was also a medical doctor and specialized in plastic cosmetic surgery and had many investments in India besides owning many hospitals in both India and Nepal. In fact, the wedding planner, Renu Jaiswal, also belonged to his group of companies. It was their specialty to do blood drives in elite weddings and donate the collected blood to a local hospital of the host's choice. That was one of the reasons Renu had become so popular as a wedding planner. Blood drives was one of the business-marketing strategies for looking different from other wedding planners by performing this noble task. They even partnered with famous organizations that would supply blood in hospitals. He told Dr. Cozee that a reporter told him about the howling and shouting of Dr. Honey Singh on the airport. Dr. Seva Shanti was always jealous of Dr. Honey Singh. He told Cozee to meet him in Taj Palace Hotel on Sardar Patel Marg, New Delhi, the next day for a buffet dinner at 8:00 PM, and he would tell him why he wanted to meet him. Cozee and Shanti were the best of friends from their residency days at the same time in Rosen Medical Center in Bethesda.

Dr. Seva Shanti was all about himself. He was a very greedy man and wanted to rule everyone globally. Although his name Seva meant Service and Shanti meant peace in Hindi. But in habits he was the total opposite of his name. He looked very calm and collected from above but he was a very messed-up man in his brain and had a gigantic ego too. He was very fair-complexioned and was six feet two inches tall. He could not see anybody rise equal and above him. Anybody's success was not an option for him. His only agenda was to rule the world by hook or crook. He even had done a stint in the Indian Army as a doctor and there he got sniper training. He was never satisfied with what he had. He was involved in shady dealings in his business and even had a money-laundering scandal linked to him. But Cozee was unaware of his shady background. Dr. Shanti wanted to settle the score with Dr. Honey Singh, as Dr. Honey Singh had debarred him during his residency program and he was not allowed to enter United States. With the help of a reputation-management firm in India he had gotten all his Internet records cleaned and nobody knew about his shady past.

Dr. Cozee's parents, Sunita and Ranveer Singh, lived in Defence Colony in New Delhi.

Dr. Cozee reached Taj Palace at eight sharp and headed towards Masala Art restaurant and saw Dr. Shanti was already waiting for him and drinking red wine. "What a pleasant surprise to see you, Cozee, after such a long time," said Shanti. "What would you like to have?"

Cozee said that he would like to have fresh-squeezed orange juice and spicy fish tikka and was in no mood to drink. The waiter was called and the food and drink were ordered. After each of them inquired about their families, the conversation shifted towards how to get revenge on Dr. Honey's family. Dr. Shanti gave so many ideas but Cozee did not like them. Shanti had done his work of inciting Cozee into taking revenge. The best would be the second-to-last idea they discussed: to spike Dr. Honey Singh's food and drinks with medicines so that whole evening he will go to the bathroom. Dr. Cozee said that this should be done only to Dr. Honey and nobody else. Dr. Shanti promised Dr. Cozee that he would do that as discussed and he would never cross this line. But knowing Shanti, he never had limits to anything. Breaking the law was his specialty and poor Dr. Cozee was caught in his spiderweb. Dr. Cozee told Dr. Shanti that his CEO, Renu Jaiswal of the wedding-planning company, was doing a fantastic job and thanked Shanti for the wonderful services they were providing in his brother's wedding. Again, Dr. Cozee emphasized to Dr. Shanti that there should be no foul play. Dr. Cozee said, "I have only given you permission to put some drug in Dr. Honey Singh's food so that he cannot enjoy the wedding and has to go to the bathroom every second."

Dr. Shanti said, "As you say, Cozee." But Shanti was bent on ruining anything related to Dr. Honey Singh. He also wanted to rule the world. He had his army of people working with him who knew what to do.

On this note they left the hotel, as it was already 11:30 PM and the next day was the Henna and Music Night.

Chapter Four:

Henna and Music Night, Dec. 24, 2018

After the daily press briefing at 4:00 PM all press was asked to stay for the Mehndi celebration in the evening in the Maurya Sheraton. There was also a special dance by Hollywood actress Angel Paul. The press was delighted to join the festivities. At 7:00 PM sharp the groom's family arrived and beautiful Las Vegas showgirls who were belly dancers were hired to receive guests with a garlanding ceremony. As the groom's side arrived they all were first sprinkled with rose water and then given garlands of red roses to wear. After these beautiful girls garlanded the guests and all the guests arrived by 8:00 PM, handsome men in tuxedos were serving appetizers, which was hot tomato soup, chicken tikka, vegetable pakoras (dumplings), as well as hot tea and coffee lattes, and in the background one could hear very soothing sitar music playing. Then the bride and groom arrived holding each other's hands, dressed as King Shahjehan and Queen Mumtaz Mahal in their elaborate outfits.

Shah Jahan, meaning King of the World, was the fifth Mughal emperor, who reigned from 1628 to 1658. Shah Jahan commissioned many monuments, the best known of which is the Taj Mahal in Agra, which entombs his beloved wife, Mumtaz Mahal, whom he loved the most among his other wives.

Dr. Jack looked extremely handsome in a long-sleeved green velvet coat called a gown with beautiful golden Zardosi embroidery. He wore a turban on the head and patka, an adorned sash, was worn on the waist. Pajama-style pants were also worn by Dr. Jack, while Dr. Rozy wore a beautiful red peshwaz-style velvet robe with heavy Zardosi or Mughal-style embroidery and churidar pants. The bride was wearing a beautiful green brocade churidar (Mughal-style pant) suit with a big dupatta (scarf) of four meters and intricate embroidery done on it matching the design of the churidar. She also wore lots of jewelry, including earrings, nose jewelry, necklaces, bangles, belts, and anklets. The jewelry had expensive and rare rubies, diamonds, emeralds, and sapphires.

The decor of the Henna and Music Night was red and green. Nisha Thakur, who had put Henna on many Bollywood celebrities as well as on Hollywood celebrities who had visited India, was booked for this occasion. She was flown from Mumbai for this Henna Night. First henna was put on fifty guests by the girls in Nisha's entourage. She was there only to put henna on the bride, Dr. Rosy. There was lots of red, green, and bling. There were red roses all around the sprawling lawn of the hotel with a beautiful chandelier in the red fort-style tent. The theme of the evening was Mughal emperor night. Besides the sitar there was Arabic music also playing in the background. The DJs were specially flown from Bollywood and they were alternating sitar and Arabic music. Also, artists playing various Mughal emperors could be seen around. One could see Emperor Akbar with his Joda Bai and King Jahangir with Nurjahan, to name a few. The mood was very festive.

After the social hour and the appetizers were served, the bride was summoned to come and sit on the stage, and she came with her bridal girls all wearing beautiful gharara pants suits in multi-colored brocades and silk. Now nobody could see Dr. Rozy's face. Her face was covered with a big yellow-and-green Punjabi phulkari flowery embroidered scarf. Rozy was also wearing rose garlands and was presented with a beautiful emerald-and-diamond set by her in-laws. Her hands and feet had been done in beautiful henna designs that morning.

After the appetizers were served, the ceremony started. All the women who came from groom's side were asked to put henna on Rosy's hand, and the henna was put on a betel leaf on her hand so that the henna that was already on her hand would not get spoiled. The Henna Night songs were playing in the background, now on a video screen. Then the artists who were hired from Bollywood came and played some henna numbers from Bollywood, which was joined by the family as choreographed by Shilpa Darling. Then the Hollywood celebrity Angel Paul performed a Bollywood number, which was the highlight of the evening.

Then the dinner was served, with typical Mughal cuisine. Mughlai cuisine consists of dishes developed in medieval India at the center of the Mughal Empire. It represents a combination of the cooking style and recipes of Central Asia and North India. The Mughlai cooking styles is used in the traditional cuisine of North India, especially Uttar Pradesh and Delhi. The exotic taste of Mughlai cuisine was made mild to accommodate international guests. One could smell a distinctive aroma and the taste of ground and whole spices. The Mughlai course was served in an elaborate buffet of main-course dishes with a variety of accompaniments. There was Haleem (Khichda) Mughlai chicken curry; a variety of tikkas, both vegetable and non-vegetarian; Mutton Biryani; Mughlai Paratha bread; minced meat and peas; Murg (chicken) Kababs; Mughlai Murgh Musallam (stuffed chicken with nuts); Pasanda Kababs; Seekh Kababs; and lamb chops. Dessert was Kulfi ice-cream, Falooda, and Gulab Jamun.

The festivities of this wonderful night came to an end at 12:00 AM on December 25, 2018. Everybody present wished everyone Merry Christmas and headed towards their hotels, guest houses, and homes, wherever they were staying. The program was hectic but very nicely arranged, was the headline in Indian papers the next day, with beautiful pictures. The excitement for the wedding increased tremendously in the hearts of the guests invited as well as the readers who had been reading about this wedding for the past several weeks. Wedding-age girls were watching these festivities very closely to incorporate some of the ideas in their own weddings if they could afford to.

Chapter Five:

Wedding Day, Dec. 25, 2018

The guests started coming at 6:00 PM, and as it was Christmas Day and the hosts were very rich, they did not want presents but instead wanted their guests to donate blood. The idea was liked by everyone. Dr. Bubleen Cozee was asked to arrange for *phlebotomists from the hospital he was practicing at. But when Dr. Honey and Baby came to know that Renu Jaiswal specialized in it, she was given an additional duty to perform.* The wedding-planning company had *a* 100% investment share from Dr. Seva Shanti. The blood-drawing company was also Dr. Seva Shanti's. Dr. Cozee also had a very successful medical-device company called Seema and Gita Medical Devices Limited, a company in the name of his daughters, and Cozee was the sole owner. They were manufacturing all kinds of medical equipment, including X-ray machines, CT-scan machines, syringes, and alcohol pads, to name a few. The syringes were supplied by this company to the phlebotomists to draw blood at the wedding. But Dr. Shanti had gotten many of his trusted people employed in this medical-device company.

One prominent name employed was the CEO of the company, Dr. Nishi Talwar, who had been the mistress and confidante of Dr. Shanti Seva for a very long time. Dr. Shanti met her in the United States when he was doing his residency. They fell in love, although Dr. Nishi wanted to get married and after finishing her residency came back to India. Dr. Nishi was from New Delhi. She had many options after finishing her residency but her love brought her back. But Shanti never married her and only gave her empty promises that he would marry her one day. Dr. Nishi was very fair-complexioned and five feet ten inches in height. She also had impeccable taste in clothes.

The quality-control head in the company was Dr. Nishi's cousin Dr. Indu Mehra, another medical graduate of Maulana Azad Medical College in New Delhi, India. On the day of the wedding the syringes were provided to the phlebotomy team by Dr. Indu Mehra. Phlebotomy means "pertaining to a blood vessel," and "cutting of" is the process of making an incision in a vein with a needle. The procedure itself is known as a venipuncture. A person who performs phlebotomy is called a "phlebotomist," although doctors, nurses, medical laboratory scientists and others do portions of phlebotomy procedures in many countries.

The wedding went very smoothly and everyone enjoyed it a lot. There were one hundred and fifty kinds of cuisine, including American, Italian, French, Mughal, Gujrati, Punjabi, Thai, and Chinese, to name a few. At 7:00 PM sharp the wedding pheras was done and the garlands were exchanged between Rosy and Jack. Hindu marriage ceremonies involve elaborate rituals, one of the most important being the "saat phere," or the seven steps to marriage. This ritual involved the bride and groom circumambulating around the sacred fire seven times while the priest chanted the holy mantras. Everyone prayed for long, happy, and blissful married life. There were artists from Hollywood and Bollywood performing. The fashion show was a big hit. All models were beautifully dressed and even invited by the President of India, Her Excellency Pheroza Motiwala, for a high tea the next day at the President's house. The models wore Misha Singh's clothes. Misha Singh was a famous designer not only in elite circles of India but also around the globe. The models wore the spring 2019 collection of Misha Singh, which was comprised of evening gowns, pantsuits, sarees, blouses, and skirts. Famous Bollywood actress Meenakshi Devi performed on Muzaffar Ali's Umraojaan's movie's song. The Hollywood actress Jisma Gomez also performed famous and scintillating Bollywood dance numbers.

After the dinner and before the entertainment started, the phlebotomy team of ten phlebotomists took blood from all who wanted to give blood. All adults present in the wedding gave blood, including the President and the PM of India. There were even one hundred pregnant women who also insisted on giving blood. The blood was sent to Mayur Hospital in Med City in Delhi, India, as Dr. Honey Singh's cousin Dr. Balwant Singh was the CEO of that hospital.

After the bidaai (the leaving of groom's side with the bride), all were very tired and wanted to sleep. As they headed towards their rooms and turned on the television, there was breaking news that the Indian Prime Minister Dr. Lakhanwala and President Pheroza Motiwala, who both attended the wedding ceremony of Dr. Honey Singh's niece, had felt dizzy in their cars while leaving the wedding and had been taken to the nearby military hospital. But the next day they became OK and were discharged from the hospital and advised to take two days of rest. Everyone thought that, as they both were in their eighties, they must be stressed.

After a week a train tour was arranged for both families to go to the Palace on Wheels, including all their international friends as well as their friends from India. The bride and groom were also supposed to join. Then symptoms of a mysterious disease were seen in everyone, including the bride and groom and anyone who attended the wedding. The symptoms were fever, rash, headache, joint pain, conjunctivitis (red eyes), and muscle pain. It was in the national and international news that some mystery illness had engulfed India, as everyone who attended the wedding of Dr. Jack and Dr. Rosy Singh was having these symptoms. The FBI (US Federal Bureau of Investigation) and CBI (Central Bureau of Investigation) were now investigating this.

Soon CBI and FBI agents were all over the wedding venue in Chatturpur Farms at Scenic View Retreat Hotel, asking questions from the hotel staff, as well as the Maurya Sheraton Hotel. There were members of Parliament from nearly all the political parties of India who attended the wedding, and they all, as well as the President and the Prime Minister of India, were having the same symptoms. The doctors said that they were infected with some kind of flu. So the trip for the Palace on Wheels was cancelled. Dr. Honey Singh had to bear lot of penalties for cancelling the trip at the last moment.

In Hollywood celebrities were also having the symptoms, along with many dignitaries in Washington, DC, who had attended the wedding. The CBI of India, in collaboration with the FBI, was now involved in investigating this mystery illness. People in Hollywood as well as in Bollywood were going berserk over this mystery illness. Dr. Honey and his whole family were put in an undisclosed destination in the USA. Dr. Honey, Baby, and Dr. Kathy, as well as Dr. Jack, Dr. Rosy, and whoever attended the wedding, were having the same symptoms. Since Dr. Honey, Baby, Dr. Kathy, Dr. Jack, and Dr. Rosy were having these symptoms, they were ruled out of any foul play and cleared of any investigation. To protect their reputation, it was announced on all media outlets that they were ruled out of any foul play and that they were also victims of this nasty act.

Interestingly, it was found that only those who gave blood were having these symptoms. It was announced that they had a suspect but for the integrity of the investigation they could not announce the name for now. Nobody knew what was happening. Even the diplomats of the embassies of the USA, Britain, France, and Italy who attended were having the symptoms. There was panic not only in Hollywood but in all of America as well as the world. Some of the celebrities who attended the wedding were pregnant and they had deformed babies.

Then only Delhi police got a call that ten dead bodies had been discovered in Lodhi Garden in New Delhi. In the autopsy it was discovered that they were poisoned by cyanide. The death time of all of them was at 3:00 AM on December 26, 2018. The bodies were all identified as the phlebotomists who had taken the blood in the wedding. So the lead agent from the CBI, who was Sheila Motwani, and the lead FBI agent, Karen Moore, came to the conclusion that this whole illness was related to blood-drawing. These two ladies were very well-known for their excellent work. As this was a high-profile investigation, they both were assigned as the lead investigator on the team with twenty agents working under them. There were ten agents from the FBI and ten from the CBI. So now the investigation was going towards that direction. Blood and urine samples were collected from everyone having the symptoms and sent for testing to the Center for Disease Control and Prevention (CDC) in Atlanta, Georgia, USA.

Chapter Six:

Mystery Illness

Many of the people infected with the mysterious illness were paralyzed, and some were on ventilators, including the Indian PM, Dr. Lakhanwala, and President Motiwala, as well as some diplomats who attended the wedding. Babies were born deformed. From one person to another, the infection was spreading like a pandemic, globally. It was already spread in India, the USA, France, Britain, and Italy. People were in panic mode. Nobody knew what was going on.

Then the test results of the blood came from CDC and it was confirmed that it was Zika virus. It was known that Zika virus was caused by a virus that was primarily spread to people through the bite of an infected mosquito. Zika mosquitoes had been found in India for many years, it was reported in various scientific journals, including *Science*, *Nature*, and *The New England Journal of Medicine*. Many people who got infected never had symptoms. In people who got sick, symptoms were of fever with rash, joint pain, or red eyes. In some the symptoms were mild, but many had life-threatening illness. Zika was also known to cause serious birth defects in babies born to women who were infected with Zika virus during pregnancy. Zika was strongly associated with Guillain-Barré syndrome (GBS), a rare disorder that could cause muscle weakness and paralysis for a few weeks to several months. GBS was an uncommon sickness of the nervous system in which a person's own immune system damaged the nerve cells, causing muscle weakness and sometimes paralysis. GBS symptoms included weakness of the arms and legs and, in severe cases, could affect the muscles that controlled breathing. GBS in some was leading to permanent damage. Zika could also spread through sex. People with Zika could pass Zika through sex to their partners even if they did not have symptoms at the time, or if their symptoms had gone away.

Adults who attended the wedding and gave blood had acute onset of fever with maculopapular rash, arthralgia, or conjunctivitis. Other commonly reported symptoms included myalgia and headache. Patients with confirmed Zika infection also developed a heart-rhythm issue and two thirds of them had evidence of heart failure.

The babies born to the ladies who attended the wedding and gave blood in the blood drive had microcephaly. Microcephaly was a birth defect in which a baby's head was smaller than expected when compared to babies of the same sex and age. Babies with microcephaly often had smaller brains that might not have developed properly. It was known that Zika virus infection during pregnancy was a cause of microcephaly. During pregnancy, a baby's head grew because the baby's brain grew. Microcephaly could occur because a baby's brain had not developed properly during pregnancy or had stopped growing after birth.

Congenital Zika syndrome was a unique pattern of birth defects found among fetuses and babies infected with Zika virus during pregnancy. Congenital Zika syndrome was described by the following five features:

- Severe microcephaly where the skull has partially collapsed
- Decreased brain tissue with a specific pattern of brain damage
- Damage (i.e., scarring, pigment changes) to the back of the eye
- Joints with limited range of motion, such as clubfoot
- Too much muscle tone restricting body movement soon after birth

Babies who were infected with Zika before birth might have damage to their eyes and/or the part of their brain that was responsible for vision, which might affect their visual development.

Both babies with and without microcephaly could have eye problems. It was also known that based on the available evidence, Zika virus infection in a woman who was not pregnant would not pose a risk for birth defects in future pregnancies after the virus had cleared from her blood. Also known about similar infections was that once a person had been infected with Zika virus, he or she was likely to be protected from a future Zika infection. Zika virus in India was very common. This meant that mosquitoes there might be infected with Zika and spreading it to people. The above symptoms were in the babies born to Zika-infected mothers. All the adults who attended the wedding and participated in the blood drive had Zika virus symptoms.

The mosquitoes that spread Zika usually did not live at elevations above 6,500 feet, (2,000 meters). People who lived in areas above this elevation were at a very low risk of getting Zika from a mosquito unless they visited or traveled through areas of lower elevation. But even people living in high elevations had Zika infection. Doctors were advising their patients that as there was no vaccine or treatment for Zika, people living in areas with Zika should take steps to prevent infection.

Infected people were asked if they had sex with condoms, which could reduce the chance of getting Zika from sex. To be effective, condoms had to be used correctly from start to finish, every time during vaginal, anal, and oral sex. People with Zika could pass Zika to their partners even if they did not have symptoms at the time, or if their symptoms had gone away. Not having sex could eliminate the risk of getting Zika from sex.

The infected people followed the CDC guidelines which clearly states that: **If your partner is pregnant use** condoms every time having sex. Everyone traveling to a Zika infected area should use condoms for the safety of their sex partners.

So it was decided that to rule out Zika virus, testing should be done according to approved CDC protocols.

So all the specimens tested from the individuals present in the wedding were positive for Zika virus and none of the people had mosquito bites. There was panic mounting in people as to what happened, and how so many people got infected with Zika virus was the question on everybody's mind. There were all kinds of conspiracy theories floating around in radio, print, Internet, TV, and social media.

#Zikavirus was trending on Twitter, Facebook, and Instagram for several days. The authorities were quiet on this subject as the investigation was ongoing.

The media was broadcasting 24/7 that anybody who had any symptoms of fever should immediately go and see their doctor and get evaluated for Zika virus, as a pandemic of Zika was suspected in this world. Because of the pandemic's uniqueness and the ability of Zika virus to harm unborn children, the pandemic had captured the attention of infectious-disease researchers and practitioners of clinical and public health medicine around the world. Researchers working on Zika virus were invited to various radio, TV, and Internet talk shows to give their insights on Zika virus.

People were in panic mode, as there was no specific medicine or vaccine for Zika virus. The doctors were prescribing the following treatment only:

- Treat the symptoms.
- Get plenty of rest.
- Drink fluids to prevent dehydration.
- Take medicine such as acetaminophen (Tylenol®) to reduce fever and pain.
- Do not take aspirin and other non-steroidal anti-inflammatory drugs (NSAIDS) until dengue can be ruled out to reduce the risk of bleeding.
- If you are taking medicine for another medical condition, talk to your healthcare provider before taking additional medication.
- If you think you may have or had Zika, tell your doctor or healthcare provider and take these above steps to protect others.
- If you are caring for a person with Zika, take steps to protect yourself from exposure to the person's blood and body fluids (urine, stool, vomit). If you are pregnant, you can care for someone with Zika if you follow these steps.
- Do not touch blood or body fluids or surfaces with these fluids on them with exposed skin.

- Wash hands with soap and water immediately after providing care.
- Immediately remove and wash clothes if they get blood or body fluids on them. Use laundry detergent and water temperature specified on the garment label. Using bleach is not necessary.
- Clean the sick person's environment daily using household cleaners according to label instructions.
- Immediately clean surfaces that have blood or other body fluids on them using household cleaners and disinfectants according to label instructions.
- If you visit a family member or friend with Zika in a hospital, you should avoid contact with the person's blood and body fluids and surfaces with these fluids on them. Helping the person sit up or walk should not expose you. Make sure to wash your hands before and after touching the person.

Chapter Seven:

Manhunt for the Suspects

Nobody knew what was going on except that the joint statement by the FBI and CBI was given that it was some kind of mystery illness, which they had now established was Zika virus, which people who attended the wedding of Dr. Rosy and Dr. Jack Singh had contracted in New Delhi, India.

The FBI and CBI also said, "We do not know how the disease was contracted in the wedding and the reason behind it. We have some people as suspects but the investigation is ongoing and so we will not announce the names of the suspects until and unless it is confirmed. The host of the wedding and their relatives are completely ruled out as suspects, including the bride and groom. They are themselves the target of this bioterrorism. We are taking it as a bioterrorism investigation. For those of you who do not know what bioterrorism is, it is terrorist acts involving the use of harmful agents and products of biological origin, as disease-producing microorganisms or toxins."

That Dr. Seva Shanti had some shady connections, both the FBI and the CBI knew, but he never used to leave any clue. Dr. Seva Shanti had been on the radar of the FBI and CBI for some years. The President Motiwala and PM Mushir Lakhanwala's health was deteriorating, and they were now proclaimed brain-dead and taken off life support by their family.

Then two FBI and two CBI agents landed at the door of Dr. Seva Shanti's house in Nepal and inquired about his whereabouts.

The house was locked but they had a search warrant. They searched the whole house but could not find any clue. There was a media frenzy as the media wanted to know what was going on. Drug-smelling dogs were also brought into the house and they could not find anything. All the money of Dr. Seva Shanti had been transferred two months back into Caribbean islands somewhere through banks in Dubai. He had sold all his properties and hospitals also. The new owners did not have a clue what was going on. They could only contribute to the investigation that they had bought these different properties of Seva through a firm by the name of Mitra Investments. When they probed to find out who the owners of Mitra Investments were in Dubai, it was found that it belonged to someone by name of Milan Chaudhry. According to UAE records, Milan Chaudhry had died ten years back. So it was a case of money laundering through underground channels. Suddenly these investigating agencies were now confronted with a mountain of complex unregulated overseas banking networks to look into.

Dr. Nishi Talwar was also nowhere to be found. Dr. Indu Mehra was found dead in a hotel in Dubai with cyanide poison in her blood. FBI and CBI agents were working around the clock to solve this case. A major percent of Dubai's investments were oil free. Many underworld kings were operating in the UAE. So now the search for the money transfer was underway.

The biggest don of the UAE was Sujan Jhunjunwala, who was involved in a lot of illegal activities. But he was also very discreet in his activities and was never arrested. But the FBI and CBI had him on their radar for many years. An FBI informant in Dubai had tipped the FBI that recently Sujan had a facelift and other cosmetic procedures done for himself and his prime associates. One of the main associates of Sujan, Miland Thappar, was arrested while throwing a lavish party in Dome Cafe for some Bollywood celebrities. Miland Thappar looked very different than before and was going to produce a movie in Bollywood. The question arose: how did Miland Thappar get the financing for this mega-million-dollar project? It was a red flag right there. When Miland was interrogated about where this money came from and was offered a deal that he would only go to prison for three months instead of life, he confessed that Sujan had recently met Shanti in Dubai and he took a cut to transfer money from India to the Bahamas. His work was to see some scripts from Bollywood to produce a film and that party was only in his name but the actual financier was Sujan. Miland had recently gotten married to his lady love, an up-and-coming Bollywood actress, Sheena Kulkarni. Miland wanted to get out of this underground business.

Miland had joined them when his boss was only in gold smuggling, wanting to make some quick bucks and marry his lady love Sheena. When his boss diversified his portfolio into drug smuggling and hired a contractor for killing people, he was very unhappy there. Sujan had threatened him with dire consequences, including the death of his lady love, and Miland wanted to get out. So Miland thought that this was a good opportunity. Miland also told the investigating authorities that Sujan and some of his associates, along with Dr. Shanti and Dr. Nisha, had plastic surgery on their faces and they looked very different now. Unfortunately Miland did not have their changed-faces photographs. Miland also confessed that Dr. Indu's food was poisoned by cyanide by another one of Sujan's men, Shridan, who worked in the Deira Luxury Hotel. Shridan also confessed to his crimes.

But there was no other connection between Sujan and these crimes except what Miland said. Although Miland's testimony was taken, Miland had no proof to prove his testimony. Sujan's attorney with their outstanding work got Sujan out of this mess quickly. Trial went for a month only. The authorities could not find any connection between Shridan and Sujan. But Shridan was given the death penalty by Dubai courts for the murder of Dr. Indu. Shridan said that he was instructed by Sujan to do this, but he also had nothing to prove his testimony. Authorities were very disappointed but they decided to never give up until and unless they solved this mystery and booked all the bad characters with the punishment they deserved. The global media was pressuring the FBI and CBI to solve this mystery ASAP.

Chapter Eight:

Funeral of PM and President of India, 2019

In the central hall of the Parliament of India New Delhi were kept the dead bodies of both PM Dr. Mushir Lakhanwala and President Pheroza Motiwala for public viewing and paying last respects.

Parliament House, or Sansad Bhavan as it is named in Hindi, was one of the most iconic and beautiful buildings in Delhi. The architects of the building were Edwin Lutyens and Herbert Baker. It was inaugurated in 1927 by Lord Irwin, the then Governor-General of India. The Parliament House was comprised of a central hall that was circular in shape and ninety-eight feet in diameter. The Central Hall was considered to be a very important part of the Parliament building, since it was here that the Indian Constitution was drafted. The building housed the Lok Sabha, Rajya Sabha, and a library hall. There was also with beautiful landscaping lay a garden. The Parliament House also had offices of the officers of the Parliament.

It was the wishes of the PM Dr. Mushir Lakhanwala and President Pheroza Motiwala that their last rites be in front of only their immediate family. Everyone had to respect those feelings. The Presidents and Prime Ministers of nearly all the countries came to pay their last respects to these two noble souls whose lives were taken by the Zika virus. There were also royalties, revolutionists, and just ordinary people. You could see tears in the eyes of many Presidents and PMs of different countries. Millions of people from India and nearby countries were pouring in to pay their last respects.

Non-resident Indians and citizens of foreign countries were going to the embassy and Consulates of India to sign the message book.

People were crying loudly as well as quietly. Some were bringing cards with a personal message. Some were bringing flowers. Both the PM and the President loved roses. So you could see nearly all kinds of roses. There was a message book kept outside the Central Hall of Parliament and people were writing their messages. The bodies of the PM and the President of India were kept till January 23, 2019, and then on January 24, 2019, they were taken for last religious rites according to the Hindu customs.

Then on Jan 26, 2019, the ashes of PM Dr. Lakhanwala and President Pheroza Motiwala were scattered in the holiest waters of India, at the confluence of the Ganges and Jumna Rivers. This spot was called Triveni Sangam, meeting place of the three rivers, which includes river Saraswati besides the above two. Every year millions of Hindus go to this place for their sacred journey place.

The scattering of the ashes of the Prime Minister and the President of India took place with full religious and military honors. A throng waded in the muddy waters of the Ganges to get a glimpse of the ceremony, which was performed by the elder sons of the PM and the President, respectively.

January 26 was specially chosen, as it was called Republic Day of India. Republic Day of India is the day on which the Constitution of India came into effect on 26 January 1950.

Chapter Nine:

Buzz about a Power Couple

There was a buzz about a new company launched in Interlaken in Switzerland by a husband and wife by the name of Mr. Aabheer Gupta and Mrs. Norain Gupta. It was called Gupta and Associates. The company took care of the logistics and all outdoor filming needs of Bollywood. Also, the company gave tours of the locations where Bollywood movies had been filmed. They gave lavish parties and paid events for Bollywood stars when they came from India to meet local people.

Interlaken a famous tourist destination in the Bernese Highlands region of the Alps. It is the main transport gateway to the mountains and the lakes in that area. The town is situated on a land named Bödeli between the lakes of Brienz to the east and Thun to the west and river Aare, flows from one end to the other. Also, there are a number of beautiful mountain resorts which are packed with tourists all around the year.. The local language is the local variant of the Alemannic Swiss German dialect.

The Guptas were new in this community but had all the contracts of outdoor shoot logistics for Bollywood. They started throwing lavish parties and inviting all the businesses and people residing in town. They even started inviting tourists to their parties. They arranged for Bollywood locale tours, both during the filming and post-filming. It's hard to imagine that this non-English-speaking country in the heartland of Europe would be synonymous with Indian cinema's fascination with romantic songs and dreamy sequences. Switzerland is a favorite destination for **immaculate backdrops**. They also had a beautiful documentary film made on the history of Bollywood in Switzerland and would play it in a theatre they had in their house, which opened primarily for business. All the shows in this theatre were always sold out.

The documentary showcased that the blockbuster film *Sangam,* of the late Indian filmmaker Raj Kapoor, released in 1964, which was nearly 200 minutes, filled with an emotional bollywood flavor of emotional scenes and songs, starring Raj Kapoor, Vyjayanthimala and Rajendra Kumar. This was the first film which was shot in international locations such as London, Vatican, Rome, Venice, Paris and Switzerland. At that time nobody, could think that Switzerland, would be one of the, favorite Bollywood locales. After that came Shammi Kapoor's thriller, *An Evening in Paris in* 1967. It was shot entirely abroad, with Paris being the main focal point. The movie also had major parts filmed in Switzerland, Lebanon and Canada. Yash Chopra, the famous Bollywood film director as well as producer, chose Switzerland as his honeymoon destination. In 1970, with his wife Pamela he took a tour of Switzerland. He was so mesmerized with Switzerland , that he filmed many of his films in Switzerland. Every Bollywood film lover had seen Switzerland in his films. So, Switzerland became a Bollywood film lover's paradise and honeymoon destination. **Bollywood packaged trips** to places like Gstaad were arranged by the Guptas' company.

Yash Chopra was nominated as the Ambassador for Interlaken. A lake where Chopra filmed many of his scenes. *Lauenensee* is now known as **Yash Chopra Lake**. A Swiss government award for rediscovering Switzerland, was given to this film director and producer. A Jungfrau Railways train was named after Chopra – an honor which not too many Swiss can claim. Interlaken, Geneva, Zürich, Bern, Gruyere, the Rhine Falls, Jungfrau, Schiltorn, Gstaad, Grindelwald, Engelberg, Titlis, Montreux, Lucerne and many of the Alpine passes happen to be the popular choices for many other Indian movie directors.

Everybody in the town started liking the Guptas a lot. Soon they were the buzz of the community. They lived in a very beautiful, luxurious, and magnificent villa which had a panoramic view of the mountains, the countryside, and the resort in the heart of the city of Interlaken. They purchased a luxurious apartment building built in 1907 and changed it to their own specifications. Nearby attractions were Jungfraujoch, Schilthorn, Tell-Freilichtspiele. Well-known ski regions could easily be reached: Wengen – Kleine Scheidegg ten kilometers, Grindelwald – First, Mürren – Schilthorn. Well-known lakes could easily be reached also. It was not only beautiful but also had historic value, and was just over a kilometer from the lake. On the ground floor they had a luxury spa for their guests and themselves. Some Bollywood stars had come along with some dignitaries from India, Nepal, and the UAE. The Guptas' company had arranged for a tour for them on the train. The train tour also included white slopes dotted with charming villages, the majestic snow-capped peaks of the Alps, and lively cities steeped in history. Switzerland was an exhilarating destination. From a scenic point of view, it was remarkable. They arranged a ride to the funicular to the top of the Klein-Matterhorn and appreciated the sheer beauty of its towering neighbor. A trip to Schaffhausen to see the spectacular Rhine Falls, the largest waterfall in Europe. The countryside beautiful view of chalets and wonderful historic castles had tourists mesmerized. Tourist destinations like Zurich, Bern, Lucerne, Basel and Lugano were also advertised in this train ride. Each of these cities have their unique flavor offering tourists modern art galleries as well as history lessons. Shopping is well-known of these destinations. Everyone knows about Swiss-made watches and so tourists were very keen on having an experience seeing how it is made. So a factory tour of a watch factory, was also added to this train ride. Skiing and snowboarding was also arranged. All of this activity made a little culinary indulgence guilt-free, with cuisine plucking dishes from neighboring France, Germany, and Italy, and hearty national specialties such as fondue, raclette and rösti. And of course, there was the chocolate shown being made on the train ride. Moreover, there was a Pakeezah movie's , famous Bollywood dance, arranged for a Saturday evening of this ten-day tour, by the famous Bollywood actress Meenakshi Devi. All the thousand tickets were sold as soon as it was advertised. But as the train was exploring the mountains on Saturday evening, there was a brawl between two of Meenakshi Devi's fans, Girdhari Sharma and Anuj

Pratap, and they were dead in a second. Police were summoned and they were both found to have cyanide in their blood after the autopsy and toxicology reports came from the forensic pathology lab in Interlaken.

The Swiss police handed this case over to the FBI, as again this cyanide-poisoning case had evolved from nowhere. As part of the investigation, everyone present in the train, including all the employees, were asked to give their blood to test DNA. Also, fingerprints were taken of everyone to see if any matched to any of the travelers or the employees and owners of Gupta and Associates. As already a lot of press had been given to cyanide poisoning in the unsolved case of the Zika-contamination pandemic earlier at a wedding in India, authorities advised all detained that there should be no press. Mr. and Mrs. Gupta also urged their clients to stay away from the press, as it would be a disaster for the reputation of their company and hence their business. The blood samples and fingerprints were sent to the FBI forensics lab in Virginia, USA.

With the widespread use of DNA testing, police, death investigators, and attorneys compared the results of the suspects and that of the forensic pathology autopsy of the victims for evidence, especially at the crime scene. As it was the cyanide-poisoning case, the same lead agent of the FBI was assigned to the case, Karen Moore. When the DNA results came they were screened for any matches. Boom: the DNA of the fingerprints on the body matched with that of Aabheer and Norain Gupta. Even the CCTV cameras on the train showed they both were near the victims when they were fighting. Also, there was match of their DNA with the DNA of Dr. Seva Shanti and Dr. Nishi Talwar in the FBI database. When they had come to the United States for the first time, their fingerprints had been taken at the airport by the immigration authorities. This was huge news not only for the FBI but also for the CBI. So Sheila Motwani was contacted by Karen Moore, and she and her ten agents flew immediately to Interlaken, Switzerland.

Chapter Ten:

Absconding Culprits Found

The FBI and CBI immediately had their warrant ready from the Swiss courts and raided the house of Aabeer and Norain Gupta, and they found two more vials of cyanide in their house. The Guptas were immediately handcuffed and taken into custody. They were asked to remain silent; anything they said could go against them in a court of law. The Guptas contacted their attorney, Kurt Shein. Kurt, after evaluating the evidence against them, told them, "I want to know whether all the evidence the FBI and CBI has against you is true or not." Kurt told them he could not do anything for them, as they would be tried in India and they would for sure get the death penalty.

The Guptas asked if Kurt could transfer their case to the United States and Kurt said he would try that. Neither Kurt nor anybody else knew why these culprits wanted to transfer their case to the USA. Perhaps it was to avoid the death penalty, as some states in the USA did not have it. Also, some cities in the USA were sanctuary cities, and they harbored illegal criminals and left them even if they had committed murders. These days there was a big uproar in the USA about sanctuary cities. Kurt was not successful in that, as their detrimental conspiracy had killed the President and the PM of India besides the citizens of the many countries involved. They asked if they could get life imprisonment instead of the death penalty, but that was also denied by the Supreme

Court of India. Kurt told them this was all he could do. Aabeer and Norain Gupta were transferred in a heavy-security FBI plane with US Federal Marshals from Switzerland to New Delhi, and they would be tried in the Supreme Court of India. Another attorney by the name of Nikhil Saxsena was assigned to them by the Supreme Court of India.

Chapter Eleven:

Confession of Crimes and Convictions

In Switzerland, Aabheer and Norain Gupta got married in a simple wedding ceremony. They were repenting for the mess they had gotten themselves into. But the crimes they'd committed could not be reversed. Dr. Seva Shanti and Dr. Nishi Talwar aka Aabheer and Norain Gupta confessed that yes, their jealousy, revengeful natures, false practices, and greed to rule the whole world had shown them this day. They gave their confession under lie detectors, aka polygraph tests. They were tired and broken from inside and were twenty-four-hour under suicide watch. They pled guilty for all the crimes they had committed. Then they confessed that as Dr. Indu Mehra was also poisoned by both of them in Dubai, the underground king of Dubai, Sujan Jhunjunwala, got this task done for them through one of his henchman, Shridan. Their confession also went like this:

First they all three, Dr. Seva, Dr. Nisha, and Dr. Indu, had poisoned the ten phlebotomists by mixing cyanide in their food, which was brought to them by Dr. Seva Shanti. These phlebotomists had to return to the hospital after taking the blood they collected from the wedding for testing. These blood-drawing specialists returned to their job in Mayur Hospital, where they all worked. Seva and Nishi also confessed that Dr. Balwant Singh, the CEO of Mayur Hospital, was also innocent.

The postmortem had already revealed that all the phlebotomists had taken food at 2:00 AM on December 26, 2018. Dr. Seva and Dr.

Nishi Talwar told them to meet in Lodhi Garden and they would deliver the food there to them. After the shift of these phlebotomists was over at 12:00 AM, they all went to Lodhi Garden as they were instructed by Seva and Nishi. They met Seva and Nishi and they hand-delivered the food, which had already been mixed with cyanide. Seva and Nishi already had a private plane arranged to get out of India and so left India after they saw that all these phlebotomists had eaten the food they delivered to them. Although Seva and Nishi were doctors who were there to save lives, they went against the oath they had taken at the time of graduating from medical school. They intentionally did this. So they were charged with first-degree murder. First-degree murder is any intentional murder that is willful and premeditated with malice aforethought.

They knew that acute cyanide ingestion would have a dramatic, rapid onset, immediately affecting the heart and causing sudden collapse. Various clinical chemistry laboratories around the globe, followed the standard protocol limit for cyanide poisoning as given here. It also could immediately affect the brain and cause a seizure or coma. >3 mcg/mL (>114 micromol/L): was detected to give death. They gave so much cyanide to them that it would be equivalent to 200 micromol/L in the blood stream. The same amount of cyanide was detected by the FBI toxicology report. They wanted to kill those phlebotomists so that they were unable to tell what actually happened. They also wanted to double-cross their friend Dr. Bubleen Cozee Singh. They asked their friend Sujan to kill Dr. Indu, as she was making lots of demands and had become a liability.

When interrogated about how much they knew about cyanide, they said they had studied this poison very carefully. They said it was a fast-acting poison that could be lethal. It is also well-known fact cited in many scientific journals and websites that it was used, as chemical weapons for the first time in World War I. Low levels of cyanides are found in nature and in products we commonly eat and use. Cyanides can be produced by certain bacteria, fungi and algae. Cyanides are also found in cigarette smoke, in vehicle exhaust, and in foods such as spinach, bamboo shoots, almonds, lima beans, fruit pits and tapioca. There are several chemical forms of cyanide. Hydrogen cyanide is a pale blue or colorless liquid at room temperature and is a colorless gas at higher temperatures. It has a bitter almond odor. Sodium cyanide and potassium cyanide are white powders which may have a bitter almond-like odor. Other chemicals called cyanogens can generate cyanides. Cyanogen chloride is a colorless liquefied gas that is heavier than air and has a pungent odor. While some cyanide compounds have a characteristic odor, odor is not a good way to tell if cyanide is present. Some people are unable to smell cyanide. Other people can smell it at first, but then get used to the odor. It is well -known fact that hydrogen cyanide has been used as a chemical weapon. Besides, this it is a well -known fact that cyanide and cyanide-containing compounds are used in pesticides and fumigants, plastics, electroplating, photodeveloping and mining. Dye and drug companies also use cyanides. Some industrial processes, such as iron and steel production, chemical industries and wastewater treatment can create cyanides. During water chlorination, cyanogen chloride may be produced at low levels. Anyone may be exposed to low levels of cyanides in their daily lives from foods, smoking and other sources. These facts many people are unaware of. Eating or drinking cyanide-containing foods may cause health effects. Also, breathing cyanide gas, especially in a poorly ventilated space, has the greatest potential for harm. Lethal exposures to cyanides result only from accidents or intentional acts. Because of their quick-acting nature, cyanides may be used as agents of terrorism. After exposure, cyanide quickly enters the bloodstream. The body handles small amounts of cyanide differently than large amounts. In small doses, cyanide in the body can be changed into thiocyanate, which is less harmful and is excreted in urine. In the body, cyanide in small amounts can also combine with another chemical to form vitamin B_{12}, which helps maintain healthy nerve and red blood cells. In large doses, the body's ability to change cyanide into thiocyanate is overwhelmed. Large doses of cyanide prevent cells from using oxygen and eventually these cells die. The heart, respiratory system and central nervous system are most susceptible to cyanide poisoning.

Many scientific journals and websites give detailed information about cyanide poisoning. If one does a research on cyanide poisoning one will find that the health effects from high levels of cyanide exposure can begin in seconds to minutes. Some signs and symptoms of such exposures are: Weakness and confusion, Headache Nausea/feeling sick to your stomach, Gasping for air and difficulty breathing, Loss of consciousness/passing out, Seizures and Cardiac arrest. The severity of health effects depends upon the route and duration of exposure, the dose, and the form of cyanide. If you have been exposed to a release of cyanide, take the following steps as is usually directed by a physician or by the emergency calls one makes: Quickly move away from the area where you think you were exposed change your location for example if indoor go outdoor and vice-versa. If indoors, shut and lock all doors and windows, turn off air conditioners, fans and heaters, and close fireplace dampers. Wash eyeglasses with soap and water before wearing. Do not use bleach to remove cyanide from your skin. If needed, seek medical attention right away. Never try to do something in panic stage. If exposed the best strategy is to call emergency services right away. Dr. Seva Shanti and Dr. Nishi Talwar also confessed that the syringes in which blood was taken were first contaminated with Zika infected blood and then repacked and used as new for drawing blood from the attendees of the Rosy and Jack Singh's wedding. These syringes were passed by quality control, as one of their accomplices, Dr. Indu Mehra, cooked the books. She was instructed by her cousin, CEO of Seema and Gita Medical Devices Limited, Dr. NishiTalwar, to do so. Dr. Seva Shanti instructed Dr. NishiTalwar to carry out this operation. Dr. Bubleen Cozee had nothing to do with it. Cozee was not part of anything and he was declared innocent.

When authorities asked how he had got Zika-infected blood. Dr. Seva Shanti confessed that some of his patients were of O blood type and he knew were Zika-infected. He took their blood for testing when they came to see him. He borrowed some blood from their vials before it was sent for testing for some additional tests. That Zika -infected blood was given to her lover Dr. Nishi Talwar to spike the syringes before taking the blood from the guests of the wedding of Dr. Rosy and Dr. Jack Singh.

As both Dr. Seva Shanti and Dr. Nishi Talwar were medical doctors, their confessions above about their knowledge of cyanide was thorough.

After leaving the wedding, Dr. Shanti Seva left for Dubai at 5:00 AM on December 26, 2018, and stayed in the Deira Towers Luxury Hotel. He flew to Dubai by hiring a private jet. He had a fake passport by the name of Durdana Singh and dressed as a Sikh man. Dr. Nishi and Dr. Indu were also dressed as Sikh men, all with fake passports.

The authorities asked where their money was, and they said that it was in a joint account in the Bahamas under the names of Durdana Singh and Sujan Jhunjunwala. Now the authorities found evidence against this don Sujan Jhunjunwala. FBI and CBI agents went to Dubai and arrested Sujan Jhunjunwala, and all his wealth of eighty billion dollars was used by India to combat drug operations in India. The authorities used the money they confiscated from Sujan to make a special task force to catch drug smugglers. With that money they also strengthened the training of the task force. Sujan Jhunjunwala was given the death penalty and his team of lawyers were unable to bargain any plea deal with the authorities in India.

So Seva and Nishi were charged with conspiracy and intention to do so. According to the Indian Penal Code, 1860, Section 299, 300 – Culpable homicide and murder – they were sentenced to the death penalty. All their wealth, which was estimated to be one hundred billion dollars, was confiscated. The death penalty was to be taken care of immediately, as ordered by the Supreme Court of India. The plea bargain of the attorney of Dr. Seva Shanti and Dr. Nishi Talwar, Nikhil Saxsena, was rejected by the Supreme Court. A commission was instituted by the Supreme Court of India to look into the matter of distributing their wealth among the victims according to their injury and the harm this unfortunate incident had caused. The foreign citizens from the USA, Britain, France, and Italy who had attended the wedding would work through their respective embassies in New Delhi to get their compensation. Anybody who was directly or indirectly harmed would be compensated according to the degree of harm.

As Dr. Honey and Baby Singh were innocent, they would be compensated too, along with Dr. Jack and Dr. Rosy Singh. Bubleen Cozee Singh and Dr. Balwant Singh were also innocent, so they would be compensated, as their business was hurt in addition to them getting infected with Zika virus. Kathy Singh and Happy Singh would also be compensated. The press conference by CBI and FBI lead agents, Sheila Motwani and Karen Moore, directly announced this along with the spokesperson of the Supreme Court, Gia Gidwani. The families of President Pheroza Motiwala and PM Dr. Lakhan Wala of India would also be compensated, as they had encountered the deaths of their loved ones. Victims who were affected by this tragedy were very happy with the judgment of the Supreme Court of India.

Chapter Twelve:

After the Judgment of the Supreme Court of India

Everyone who was affected by this sighed a sigh of relief after the judgment of the Supreme Court of India. Now Dr. Honey Singh, Dr. Baby Singh, Dr. Kathleen Singh, Dr. Happy Singh, Dr. Bubleen Cozee Singh, Dr. Jack Singh, Dr. Rosy Singh, and Helen were released from the unknown destination they had been taken to by the authorities. They had been taken to the undisclosed destination to prevent any harm being done to them by the bad characters or by anyone who was affected by this tragedy. They were allowed to go back home and resume their normal, routine work.

By God's grace now Dr. Jack and Rosy Singh were parents of twins, a beautiful girl by the name of Chitra Singh and a handsome boy named Taimur Singh. Also, these babies were healthy. It was a miracle that they did not get Zika virus, and nobody had an explanation for that. Dr. Honey and Baby Singh, through their Honeybabe Foundation, donated three billion dollars to those victims who had encountered death or any kind of disability from Zika virus. They also donated five billion for Zika research to the National Institutes of Health.

Dr. Jack and Rosy threw a lavish party to welcome their newly born babies at Gaylord National Resort & Convention Center at the Potomoc River.

The invitations were first given to all those people who came to the wedding of Dr. Jack and Rosy Singh and were affected by Zika. Hollywood celebrities, including celebrity authors, were also invited. The cuisine of the party was American prepared by celebrity chef Martin Luizo. Luizo was very famous globally for his cuisine. Luizo even had a food reality show he judged on Food Network. Luizo was a best-selling author of many cookbooks on American cuisine. The cuisine of the United States also showcased its history. People who settled in United States from Europe introduced, a variety of various ingredients, spices, herbs and cooking styles. There were many dishes, including lobsters, special salads, New York strip steak, veggie burgers, chicken burgers, French fries, mashed potatoes, special meatloaf, Reuben sandwiches, apple pie, pecan pie, and chocolate and vanilla cakes, to name a few. There were also many kinds of special non-alcoholic drinks. He cooked the same menu he had cooked for famous Hollywood star Liz Shaw's wedding.

Hollywood actress Jean Robert danced on a scintillating Bollywood number. The invitations they had sent said no presents. They instead wanted the money from the guests to go to Dr. Featherson's NIH research group, which was working very hard to get a vaccine for Zika virus. Dr. Featherson and his group from NIH, the main researchers on Zika virus, were invited. Dr. Featherson was asked to tell the audience about Zika virus and how far they were from developing a vaccine against this deadly virus. The party came to an end at 2:00 AM and everyone present enjoyed it a lot.

Chapter Thirteen:
Multi-Million-Dollar Deals

Dr. Honey and Baby Singh's Honeybabe Foundation produced a movie on Zika virus with a very famous Hollywood documentary director, Barbara Wilkinson. All the doctors in Honey Singh's practice also announced that they would see all the patients of Zika free of cost. So Kathy, Jack, and Rosy Singh also vowed to see Zika patients free of cost.

Hollywood producers and agents were contacting Dr. Jack and Dr. Rosy Singh to write a script for a Hollywood movie to be made on their personal experience when this Zika-virus tragedy broke. A reality show on Zika virus was already signed by them for the Science Channel.

They also got a multi-million-dollar book deal by a very famous publisher to write their personal experience, how Jack and Rosy felt when this Zika-virus tragedy broke. Jack and Rosy had already started writing this book. The book's name was *Zika Virus, A Monster: A Personal Experience*. They also signed a contract with a Hollywood producer by the name of Steve Berger who was very famous around the world.

For Dr. Honey and Baby Singh and their families in the USA and India, adversity and challenging times changed to happy days once again.

<u>Photo #1, 2, and 3:</u> As I have written earlier, President Trump has always inspired me. I am so happy that he is our President. The silent majority like us loves and respect him a lot. May God Almighty always bless him Amen/ Ameen. I celebrated the victory of him becoming President by throwing a victory party for some friends in honor of him becoming our President.

<u>Photo #4:</u> All my teachers are always very special to me. Here I visited my school in India with one of my teachers whom I respect and love a lot.

<u>Photo #5 and 6:</u> I was invited to give a book presentation of my best-seller and hot #1 new-release book on the Coalition for Trump Victory Cruise in 2017.

Photo #7, 8, 9, and 10: On a book tour.

Photo #11, 12, 13, 14, 15, 16, and 17: I love fashion and doing fun activities that keep my creative juices flowing.

Photo #18 and 19: *Merry Christmas and Happy New Year celebration with my hubby (Photo #18) and with my TV show executive producer, Nilima Mehra (Photo #19) extreme right.*

About the Author: Dr. Afshan Naheed Hashmi

Dr. Afshan Naheed Hashmi was born in India and educated in both India and the USA. Dr. Hashmi is an author, award-winning entrepreneur, speaker, and educator; a book, movie, make-up, and beauty-products reviewer; a film critic and radio and TV host; and a successful regulatory, business-development, and scientific professional with more than a decade of experience. Dr. Afshan Naheed Hashmi is also a member of the Republican National Committee Presidential Advisory Board since 2017 to present. She is Charter Member of Trump Make America Great Again Committee 2018.She is also a Republican National Committee member since 2016 to present.

Author: http://afshanhashmi.com/
General: http://drafshanhashmi.com/

<u>Thank You and Request to Readers to Give a Review for _The Outbreak of a Monstrous Infection_</u>:

First of all, I am very thankful to all of you for making my first book, _The Modern Mughal Mentality: New Strategies to Succeed in India and the Global Marketplace_, a best-seller and hot #1 new-release in a category on Amazon. I am extremely grateful to all my readers and fans who have given me an honest review for _The Modern Mughal Mentality_.

Now that you have read my second book, _The Outbreak of a Monstrous Infection_, please do not forget to give an honest review. Also, readers, please help me in spreading the word about my books in your networks.

More books from me are on your way, so keep looking for them! Please follow me on my social media platforms. All details on my website.

If you want to contact me, please contact me through email:
afshan@drafshanhashmi.com

Cheers and best wishes from your loving author!
Dr. Afshan Hashmi
http://afshanhashmi.com/
www.drafshanhashmi.com/

Bye-bye for now!